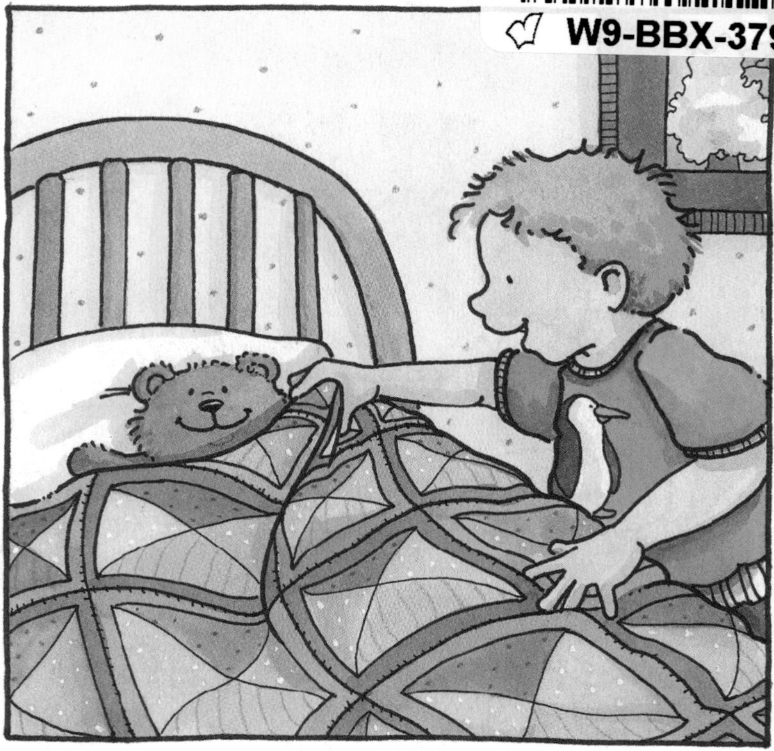

My bear can sleep.

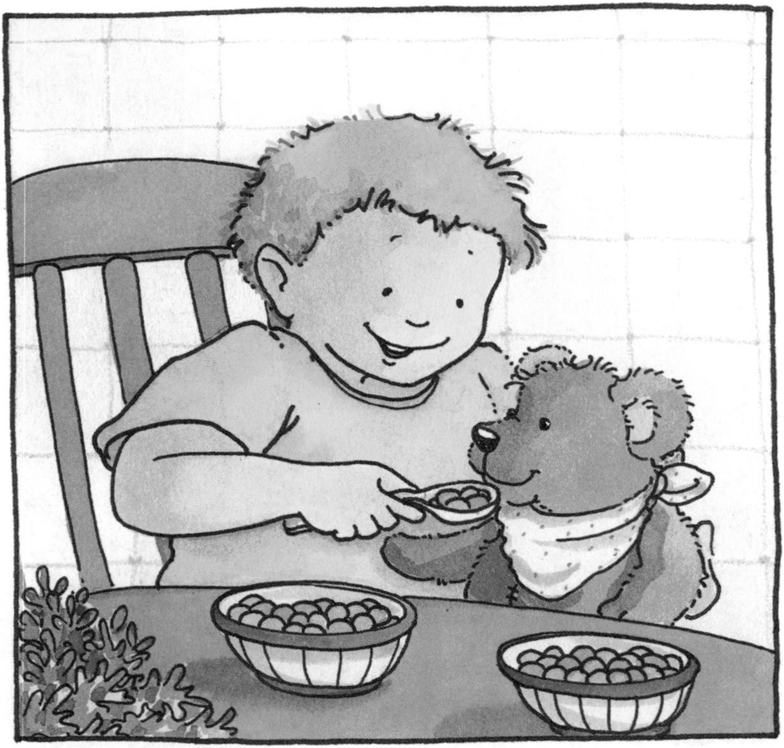

My bear can eat.

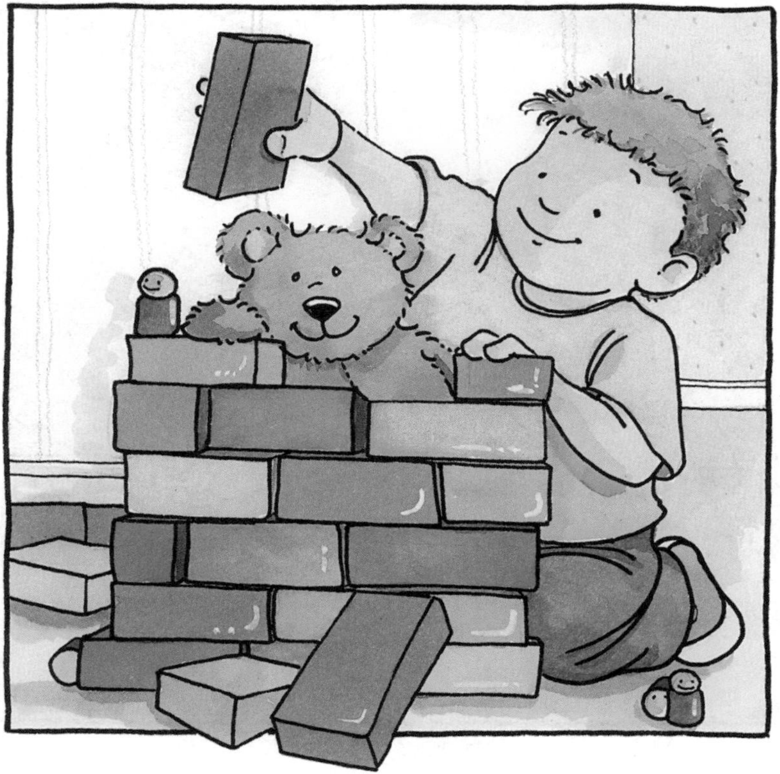

My bear can play.

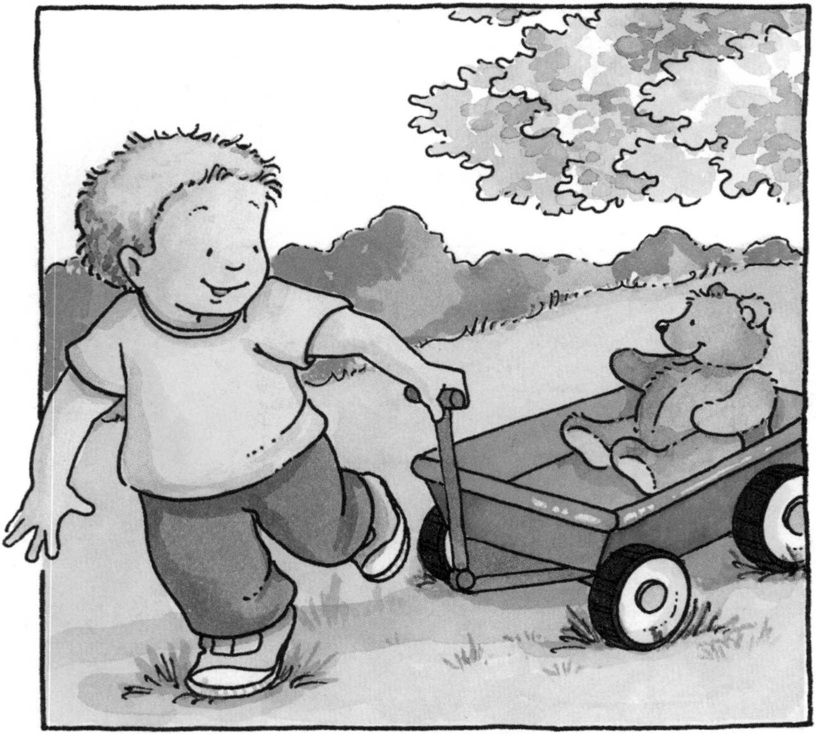

My bear can ride.

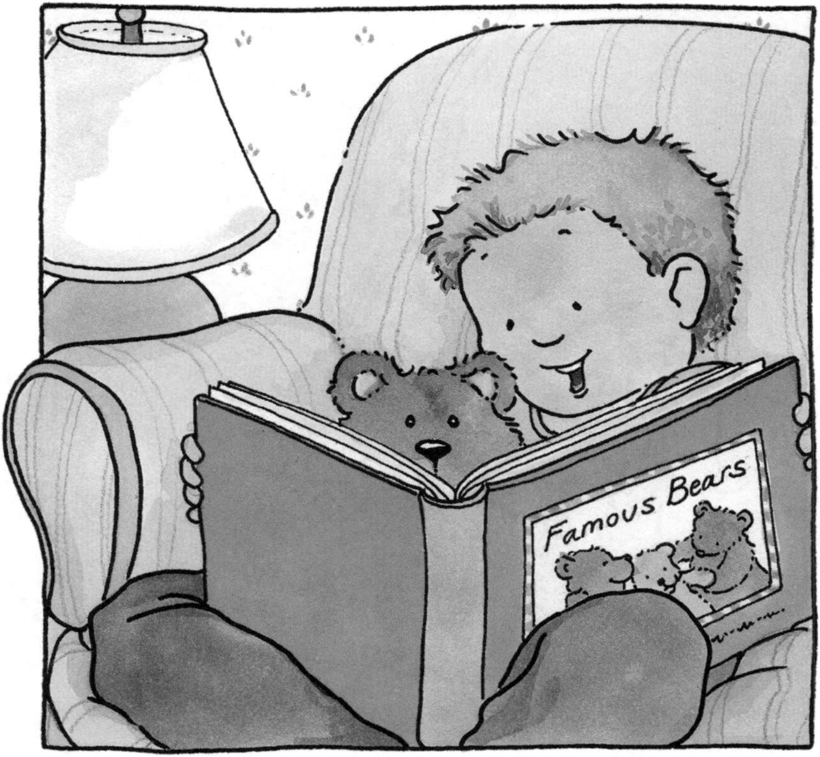

My bear can read.

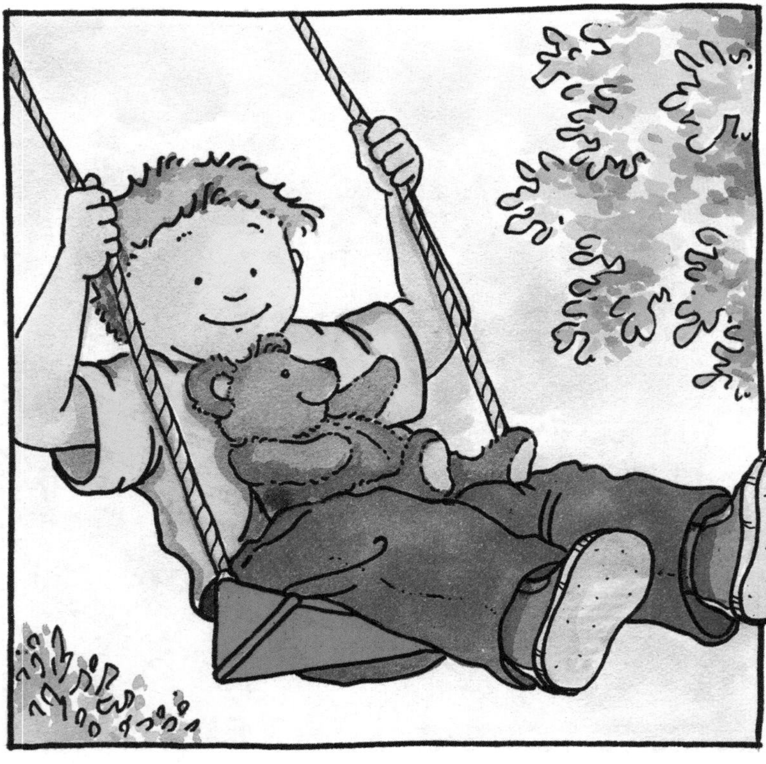

My bear can swing.

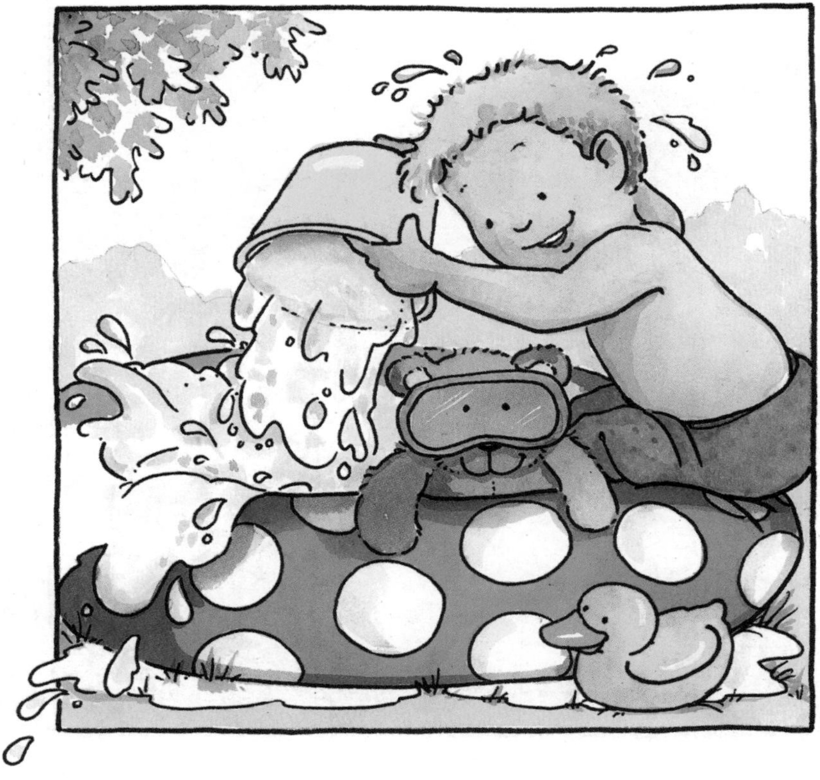

My bear can swim.

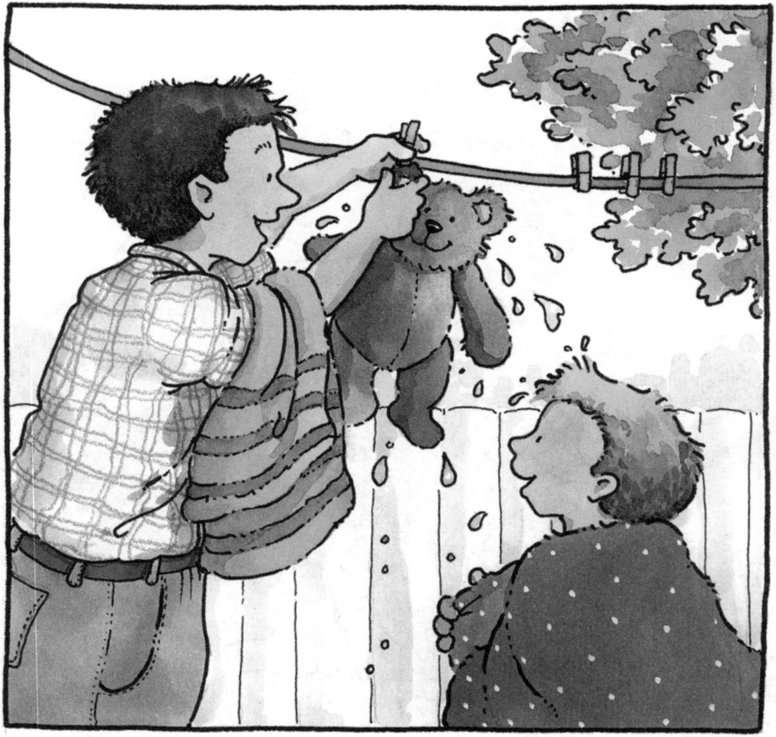

My bear can dry!